They See Me and Other Haunting Stories

Stephanie Anne

Published by Stephanie Anne, 2022.

This is a work of fiction. Similarities to real people, places, or events are entirely coincidental.

THEY SEE ME AND OTHER HAUNTING STORIES

First edition. January 18, 2022.

Copyright © 2022 Stephanie Anne.

ISBN: 979-8215713181

Written by Stephanie Anne.

Table of Contents

To my husband, Mark.

I could write something mushy and romantic about how loving and supportive you are, but I think we both know how we would feel about that.

Love you, Babe

Introduction

Why, hello there, Dear Reader,

I hope you're doing well. If you've picked up this book, one can only assume that you are hoping to encounter shadowy figures with sinister motives. Perhaps you feel more comfortable experiencing monsters in this way. You can sit in your favourite comfy chair, safe in your own home with the knowledge that the ghosts contained within these pages cannot rise up and out into the world beyond this collection. But I'm sorry to say that there are monsters all around us. You may have already seen them before. Some are even human.

So, take a deep breath, enjoy whatever lingering pleasant feelings you can, and brace yourself. The only words of encouragement I can offer you are these: don't be scared, and don't let the monsters see you.

Enjoy!

Much love,
    Stephanie Anne

The Screams

It's happening again. I wake up screaming.

Without warning, my body jerks itself violently awake from a dreamless sleep, and the screams are coming out of my mouth before I even know what is happening. Mentally, I am probably still half asleep, but I am still just aware enough to be very worried. When the screaming stops, I pause and listen for any unusual sounds, any indication that there is someone nearby who heard me. All I can hear is the frantic beating of my own heart.

When the beating slows to a more manageable pace, I settle down into the back seat of the car, scratching in places where I imagine I must have been bitten by fleas. Although I am all curled up once more, my body is stiff and my ears are alert. Someone could still be out there waiting, listening. When what felt like enough time passed, I allow my body to get a little more comfortable, although I am certain that was the end of my rest. Miraculously, I manage to fall back asleep, but the sleep that follows is restless and filled with feverish dreams.

When I wake up next, there is a bit of lightness passing through the dust clouds in the sky. It might be morning, but it is always hard to tell. The dust clouds block out all of the sun, so unless you can find a watch or a clock that still works, it's impossible to discern what time of day it is. Not that those kinds of details matter much anymore. Day or night, everything is the same.

Still shaken by my screaming in the night, I crawl out the window of the old car and begin to put some distance between myself and the highway. It is a miracle no one has come for me in the night. The highway is always a good place to seek refuge, so there is almost always someone else nearby, sleeping in another broken down car. I can't see anyone, and I can't see any signs that anyone else might be nearby, but I don't exactly feel like I am all alone either. The skin on the back of my neck prickles, and I scratch it away. I break into a run.

I only stop running when I am out of breath and drenched in sweat. There is a foul odour drifting on the wind, and I can't tell if it is me or not. It probably is.

By the time my run slows to a walk, just outside of a half-destroyed gas station, I realize that running would have only made things worse if anyone was watching me. If I hadn't screamed, I would have had no reason to run. Running marked me as a guilty person. Still panting, I look around again but still can't see anyone. It doesn't look like I was followed, and it doesn't look like anyone saw me running. I am at least safe for now. But I have to keep my head on a swivel.

I'm not expecting to find much in that old gas station. It looks as if looters and passersby already had their way with it. That is usually the case these days. But I figure it won't hurt to check for supplies anyway. You never know. Besides, what else is there to do around here?

Just about every shelf is empty, and there are traces of human excrement on the floor. The corners reek of days-old piss. I check in every nook and cranny and find nothing. None of this surprises me, and I'm not all that distressed. Last time I had a chance to stock up on supplies, I did well for myself. And I have learned how to properly ration my findings, so my pockets are still fairly full. Instinctively, I pat my jacket pockets to confirm what I already know.

I walk around the gas station one more time, just in case, and I realize that I am still sweating profusely. I try to tell myself that I am just overheating in the small space. It is because of my run, because of my jacket. That has to be it. But I won't take my jacket off because I can't risk parting with my hard-earned supplies. I will risk the sweats, instead.

After final confirmation that there is truly nothing there for me in the gas station, I step outside, pick a random direction, and walk. My heart skips a beat when I notice another person off in the distance, walking down the highway towards the gas station from the direction I came from. They don't seem to notice me, and enough time has passed that I am pretty sure they hadn't seen me running.

I tell myself that I have nothing to fear. I have only been screaming because of stress, that's all. I am just under a lot of stress. I keep telling myself that over and over as I walk away from the gas station, keeping the corner of my eye on the other person the whole time. I can't give them a reason to kill me. I can't give them a reason to think that I might have The Screams.

No one knows how the virus came to be. It made an appearance when the first of the dust clouds began to cover the Earth after the Great Drought. Some people think that the dust clouds caused the virus. Others think it was all just a coincidence that both events began to terrorize the Earth around the same time. Either way, it doesn't really matter anymore. There isn't a solution for either catastrophe, and there likely never will be.

Everyone calls it The Screams because of what it does to you.

It starts off small. You wake up screaming in the middle of the night. And by the end, you're screaming all the time. No one knows why. No one knows if The Screams are caused by pain, or if the virus simply presses all the wrong buttons in your brain. The only thing anyone really knows about it is that it's highly contagious and very deadly. If you stumble across someone who's got a case of The Screams, it's better just to kill them right away. That's why it's best to avoid people these days. Especially people with weapons.

There are other side effects of the virus to look out for. They indicate a case of The Screams long before the unlucky individual dies wailing, spewing foamy and infected blood out of their eyes, mouth, and nose. There's sweating, itching, and dark blue bruising that covers the whole body. But the screaming always comes first.

I do a symptom check every now and again, just to make sure I don't have it. I know I don't, but it never hurts to be certain. Sure, I'm sweating more than usual, but that's only because I'm wearing this thick coat with all of its wonderful storage pockets. I doubt I'll ever take it off. And yes, I'm itchy all the time, but that's only because I have lice or fleas. Or both.

I've been living outside for so long and haven't had a bath in ages. What else could it be? The bruises are just from a scavenging trip gone wrong. I fell down a flight of stairs. I think. I can't actually remember anymore. But the screaming is definitely just from stress. I'm under a lot of stress all the time now, especially since it's getting harder to find supplies and even harder to find people who don't want to kill you. It's just stress.

The person I saw on the highway is still walking in my direction. I'm certain now that I'm being followed. They walked right past the gas station and didn't even both to check for supplies. They must think I have The Screams. They're wrong, they just don't know it yet.

I can't tell for sure, but maybe they're getting closer. I tell myself that it'll be all right. I don't actually have any symptoms. I can't. It's not possible. I've checked myself thoroughly. Besides, there's a perfectly logical explanation for everything that's happened to me, so I'll just explain that to them when they catch up. They can't argue with the facts. They won't kill me when I explain to them that I don't have The Screams.

Is that a gun?

They See Me

"Morning, ghost family."

I walked right through the mother while she sliced apples for her toddlers. She didn't notice. Neither did anyone else in the kitchen. They only turned to look when I grabbed a snack from the fridge. Their usual incomprehensible chatter stopped, and all eyes turned towards me. One of the children cried.

Out of all the ghost families I've ever lived with, this one is the most hostile towards me. They don't like sharing what they think is theirs.

I've been able to see ghosts for a long time now. They're not at all like I thought they would be. I was expecting fleshless spectres, floating through spaces, leaving cold air in their wake. Colourless, lifeless, devoid of all recognizable aspects of humanity. But real ghosts are nothing like what you see in the movies. They're alive in their own special way. Ghosts think they're alive, so they act alive. And they look normal. Watching them go about their day is like watching an ordinary person. They might as well be my roommates. The only difference is that they exist on another plane. It's like I'm watching them through a pane of frosted glass.

I had an accident many years back, and I've seen them ever since. They were there when I came home from the hospital. At first, it was shocking to see strangers in my house. They looked so alive to me then, and I didn't know any better. I yelled and I screamed, but they didn't notice me at all. I tried to touch one, and my hand passed right through them. But my skin was buzzing with electricity afterwards. Remnants of life that clung to their souls, perhaps.

I quickly realized what they were, and they didn't scare me after that.

Besides, they don't bother me. They exist in their own separate dimension and leave mine alone. Well, sometimes they move the furniture around, or put things where I can't find them, but that's a minor inconvenience. They really don't bother me. And I don't bother them. They aren't even aware of me. They simply pass through, living their lives in the ways they used to when they were alive.

I've tried talking to them, but they can't hear or see me. Now, I only talk to them for my own benefit. I don't go out as much as I used to. Not since the accident. These spirits are the closest thing I have to regular human interaction.

"'Scuse me. Just going to go back to my room. No need to worry, I'm out of your way now. The kitchen is all yours. Oh, of course you have to touch the fridge now that I've touched it. Clever. Very clever. I'm sure you'll figure it out eventually."

I feel bad for them. Those poor, lost souls, clinging to their memories and the lives they once had, living in a never-ending loop. They don't seem to be aware of anything else outside of this cycle. Apart from this latest group, nothing I do pulls them out of their routine. It gets hard to watch after a while. What's the point of such a sad existence?

I've attempted talking to them in the hopes that I can help them find peace. I don't know if there even is an afterlife for them to go to, but I feel compelled to do what I can to help them move on. This can't be all there is, and there has to be a reason they're stuck here in my home.

"There are plenty of other nice homes on this block," I've told more than a few of them. Unfortunately, that doesn't get them to move on any faster.

Shortly after my accident, I tried talking to a little girl. I mean *actually* talking to her. She was one of the first ones I saw, and I cried when I thought of how young she must have been when she died. When I spoke to her, I felt as if she could see me, so I thought I could get through to her with enough effort. She got a funny look in her eye when I was near her, and she scrunched up her little face like she was trying to figure it out. But she never really looked at me. She was always looking right past me, or right through me. She knew I was there but couldn't see me.

Out of all of the ghosts I've tried to talk to, she was the one I made the most progress with. There have been others, but they stare right past me, or cock their heads as if listening for some far-off sound. But communication with these spirits never works, no matter how hard I strive. I gave up after a while and just let them be.

One thing that puts my mind at ease is that they do move on after a while. I haven't been able to figure out what actually causes this. One day, they're just gone.

Maybe, after enough time in their loop, they realize that they are no longer living and that there is nothing left for them in their meaningless routines. Maybe then they're able to move on to some sort of an afterlife. Or maybe they keep wandering through their old routines until their memories fade away. They get to the point where they no longer know who they are, and they simply cease to be.

The uncertainty gives me chills. Even worse is the realization that someday that will be me. I try not to think about it. But an image of that little girl still pops into my mind.

"I can't wait until you lot move on," I called down the stairs to the current group of ghosts. "If you need any help with that, let me know."

New ghosts always emerge, though, as if to take the place of the ones before. I don't know why they pick this place. There's nothing particularly special about it. At least, I don't think so. Maybe it has nothing to do with this place at all. Maybe it's me. I must give off some kind of energy that attracts them. I don't mind it, though. Not really. If there's something about my presence that gives them comfort in this sad state of an afterlife, then I'm just glad I can make them feel better about their situation.

This new group is more stubborn, though. They're different. And they don't want to leave. I don't think they can see me, but they at least sense that I'm there, almost like that little girl. They look right at me, but their eyes don't quite latch on. They must see me through the same pane of frosted glass that I see them through. To them, I'm there, but not really present.

And these ghosts are more aggressive. They must have been terrible people when they were alive. Or it could be that their spirits are restless because they died under violent circumstances. Either way, these ones are obnoxious. Borderline poltergeists. They believe that they have more of a right to my house than I do. They've been doing everything in their power to get me to leave.

"No need to chase me. I'm locking myself in my room. Kitchen's all yours if you want it. I won't argue with you today."

But I'm not leaving. This is my house. My home. I have been kind enough to welcome the ghosts into my personal living space. They have no right to try to force me out. And I've lived with ghosts for long enough that nothing scares me anymore. Nothing they do has any effect on me, and their little tantrums are easy to ignore. When things are moved or disturbed, I brush it off like nothing's happened.

"Do your worst! I dare you!"

Unfortunately, not everything is so easily ignored.

I drew the line when I started breaking out in a rash. I don't know how, but I knew that they were the cause. I've tried to communicate with them – genuinely communicate – in the hopes that if I can help these spirits find peace, they'll leave me alone. I should have known better. Communication with ghosts never works.

They see me now, just as I see them. And we hate each other. When I'm near them, my skin burns – not just from the rash they've given me. They scream and throw things at me. It's impossible to get any rest. If I retreat into another room, they follow me. This is the first time I have ever retaliated against the ghosts. What they do to me, I do to them tenfold.

Once our turf war begins, it's not long until there's a new ghost with them. They brought in reinforcements. That is the moment that I falter. Looking at him makes my stomach tighten in knots. He looks familiar, but in an unfamiliar sort of way. It's as if I've never seen him before, but I've seen ghosts *like* him.

"Who's this?" I say uncertainly, trying to sound tougher than I am. "How were you able to get reinforcements from the spirit world if you can't even move on?"

The foreboding sense of recognition makes me nauseous. And his actions confuse me. He is different than any of the others I have ever seen before. He doesn't move out of routine. He moves with a sense of *purpose*. He walks through my house chanting strange phrases, throwing water on everything.

"...*Adjure te, spiritus nequissime, per Deum omnipotentem...*"

Crosses appear on my walls.

And then I know.

My stomach churns as the realization hits me with the same weight and intensity that I felt all those years ago. It's like getting hit by that car all over again.

This man is a priest.

They are not poltergeists or ghosts. None of them have ever been ghosts. This is not my home. It's *theirs*.

The priest looks me dead in the eye.

"I'm the ghost?"

I should have seen the signs. It was all right there. *I* am the one who's been haunting *them*.

And now they see me.

And I'm alone. Utterly alone. With nowhere to go. I don't even know if I *can* go.

What happens if the priest succeeds? Will he kill me, or force me to go somewhere else? And what happens now that I know what I am? Will I be able to move on to an afterlife? *Is* there an afterlife? Will I fade away until I've completely disappeared? What is going to happen to me?

I need more time to figure this out. More time in this house.

I'm scared.

Ex

"What do you think?"

"What do I think of what?"

"Well, it's sad, isn't it?"

She stared for a moment at the scene in front of her, not really feeling any particularly strong emotions one way or the other. Maybe she was supposed to feel sad, or something, but she didn't.

"I guess it is."

"And I think it's scary."

"Oh, yeah?" She didn't really care to know why. She was just being polite.

Her co-worker nodded. "That could have been one of us."

She shrugged. "Probably not."

"But what if it had been you or me here working late instead of Jen?"

She looked back at their manager's body, lying a few feet away behind police tape. There was blood everywhere, and a knife was sticking out of her chest. Since the body hadn't been sent to the coroner yet, no one knew for sure how many times Jen had been stabbed. She guessed eight.

"Well? Did you hear me, space cadet?"

"Yeah. I was just thinking. Jen was stabbed a lot. I don't think this was random. We would have been fine."

"Oh. Oh! You think it might be Jen's ex?"

She shrugged.

They waited off to the side for the police to question them while her co-worker blabbed on about Jen's old relationship and how they all should have seen the red flags. But she wasn't listening. She watched intently as the body and surrounding area were examined. The knife was dusted for fingerprints, but by the way the police were shaking their heads, it didn't look like any were found. Not any usable ones, at least. She was almost surprised by that. But not really.

By the time they took the body away, there was someone questioning her co-worker, and she turned her attention towards their conversation instead. Her co-worker was a blubbering mess by this point. Embarrassing. The police officer remained calm.

She supposed he was attractive, but that didn't really mean anything. It was easy for her to find other people attractive, and she was the victim of frequent crushes. The last one did not end well for her. Although she didn't understand most emotions, she felt love fiercely. With no other feelings to get in the way, she could love in a way no one else could. But that was often her downfall. It certainly was last time. She had confessed her feelings too soon and was rejected. With her fingernails digging into her palms, she told herself not to fall for the police officer. But when he finished questioning her co-worker and began to move towards her, she could feel another crush coming on.

"Morning. I'm Detective Wellington," he said with a warm smile. She knew instantly that she was doomed.

"Morning," she said as coldly as she could. She didn't want to seem too interested or too desperate. That's usually what drove people away: the reek of desperation and loneliness that hung about her like a perfume.

"You were the second employee to arrive this morning, correct?"

"Yeah, I stayed late to help close up last night, so I was a little late getting here this morning. By the time I got in," she said, nodding to her co-worker, "the police had already been called."

"So, you were here last night? With Jen? You might have been the last person to see her then."

"Maybe." She shrugged. "I guess. I left first, so I don't know if anyone came in after."

"Your colleague mentioned an abusive ex. Do you think he would have come by?"

"Who knows. Jen told me she had been thinking of going back to him. I told her it was a mistake."

"I see."

Detective Wellington asked her a few more questions about their workplace environment, Jen's relationships with her employees and her ex. She tried to answer as best she could, but she kept getting distracted. She kept getting lost in his eyes. They were blue, her new favourite colour.

"Well, this has been a lot for you to deal with this morning," the detective said as he slipped his notebook into his pocket and took out a card. "If you think of anything else, please call me."

When he said that, her normally-still heart skipped a beat.

* * *

Work was closed down for a couple of days while the crime scene was cleaned up. She spent much of that time sitting around her apartment, starring at the card Detective Wellington had given her. She kept racking her brain, trying to come up with reasons to call him. There wasn't anything else about Jen that would be useful to him. And she knew he wasn't interested in her; he had only given her his phone number because of Jen. But still, the fact that he had given her his number at all felt like it meant something. It had to.

By the time her workplace reopened, she had an idea. She used her last heartbreak as inspiration. But this time, she was determined to make things would work out in her favour.

After closing up at the end of that first day back, she waited until she was the last one left before making the call. She was a horrible actress, and an even worse liar, but she tried her best to sound scared when Detective Wellington answered the phone.

"I'm just so scared that what happened to Jen will happen to me," she said. She tried to make her voice tremble but was unsure of whether or not she was actually succeeding. "Can you please come and stay with me while I close up? You don't even have to come inside. You can just wait by the door. Please?"

"Okay. Okay. Try to stay calm. Take a deep breath."

"I just can't be here alone right now!" She made sure to keep interrupting him. She couldn't give him a chance to say no.

"I'll…" he sighed. "I guess I can be there in…five minutes. Are you going to be okay to wait that long until I get there?"

"I think so." She lost her focus on her fake tremble when her lips curved into a smile. It didn't matter. He believed her, and he was on his way.

When he arrived, she opened the door for him before he could decide whether to wait outside or not. She needed to be close to him.

"Thank you so much."

"You're welcome. You know, I tried to explain over the phone, but I think you might have been a little too…upset, and I don't think you heard me. We do have a suspect in custody, so you're perfectly safe."

"Thank you," she said. As an afterthought, she added in a mock sigh for good measure. "That makes me feel a lot better."

"Her ex didn't have an alibi for that night, and everyone we interviewed seemed to think that he wanted to hurt Jen for breaking up with him. We're questioning him now."

"That's good." She moved closer to him. And then closer. She could smell his cologne.

"Yes, very. So, you see, this is all being handled, and you really have nothing to fear."

"I'm glad," she said. She forced her biggest and best smile onto her lips. "You caught a suspect really fast. You must be very dedicated to your job."

"Yeah," he chuckled. "My wife thinks I'm a little *too* dedicated."

"Oh. You're married?"

"Yup. Six years next month. And I'm still crazy about her. Although, I probably drive her a little bit crazy," he added with a laugh.

She sighed and reached into her pocket. Another heartbreak.

"You're just like Jen," she said.

"Excuse me?"

"You can't see a good thing when it's standing right in front of you. You can't see that you're with the wrong person and that there's someone better waiting for you."

He had a puzzled expression on his face that she didn't understand. He looked exactly like Jen right now, standing in the same spot, with the same confused look on his face. Why was love so difficult for everyone else to understand? Just like Jen, he just didn't understand what real love could be. Neither one of them would ever understand what they were missing. What a pity. There was only one way to make him understand.

His eyes widened before she even pulled out the knife.

"It was you."

Costumier

Mary wiped the sweat from her brow but froze mid-motion. Her heart pounded in her throat as she carefully peeled her hand away and examined it, fearful of what she might find. Colourful pigments mixed with the sweat that clung to her skin. She had smudged her makeup. The ensuing surge of anxiety was enough to send her over the edge. She already came down with a case of stage fright earlier in the day, but now that her makeup was ruined, she was experiencing full blown panic.

"Help." It was barely a whisper. "Help! Makeup!" she called a little louder when she found her voice.

"Oh, dear. Now, what seems to be the matter?" the costumier said sweetly as she shuffled over.

She looked so frail that Mary wondered how the old woman was able to do this job for so long. All of the women who worked as costumiers were very, very old, but this one was particularly advanced in her years. It was astounding. These women had dedicated their lives to this annual festival and had seen so many wonderful performances over the years. Mary worried that she looked like an amateur by comparison with her ruined makeup. And she worried that she wouldn't do a good job with her performance. A second wave of cold sweat came, and her heart was beating so loud she was sure the old woman could hear it. The stage fright had returned with a vengeance.

"Oh, dear. Your makeup's all smudged," said the costumier before Mary even opened her mouth. "We can fix that up in no time."

"I-I'm the third o-one," said Mary. She tried desperately to calm herself, taking what she thought were deep breaths. It wasn't working.

"Oh, dear. Not to worry. Not to worry. The performances haven't even begun yet. The guests are all still at the banquet. There's plenty of time to get you prettied up. Besides, three is a lucky number. All will be well."

Mary let the older woman take her by the hand as they walked over to a little makeup table. Those soft, leathery hands were comforting but did little to alleviate the severe case of stage fright.

"Oh, dear. You're trembling. Just take a moment to breathe, and it will all be fine."

Mary took her advice and took a nice, deep breath, a real one this time, tightening her grip on the old woman's hand for good measure. The breath wavered as it passed through her lips, but Mary's breathing was steady again by the time she emptied her lungs.

"There you go, dear."

Wasting no time, the old woman set to work. With steady hands, she reapplied the brightly coloured paints to the areas that were smudged. Mary considered herself very lucky to be wearing these paints. Only the performers were allowed to wear such bright colours. Even her dress was more brightly coloured than what she was used to wearing. She felt like a rainbow in this soft and luxurious dress. No, she felt like a queen.

Her look, and that of the other two performers, had been carefully designed to make her stand out. Their Lord needed to be able see them from wherever he was. It was a stark contrast to the appearances of the other women in the theatre that night. All of the costumiers and priestesses could only wear drab and modest grey. This particular costumier, however, now had bright smears of colour on her fingertips from fixing Mary's makeup. And, true to her word, the old woman was finished in no time.

She sat back and admired her handiwork.

"Perfect. Absolutely perfect. Our Lord will be pleased. You're still nervous, dear?"

Mary nodded. The old woman crossed her hands in her lap and thought for a moment. Her wrinkled lips pursed occasionally before she opened her mouth to speak.

"Don't tell the Mother Priestess, but I'm very jealous of you right now," said the old woman.

A giggle escaped Mary, and she fought to hold it back.

"Yes, I know, dear. I am a wicked old woman for succumbing to such a sin when I have taken my vows and lived by them for so many years. But you are a *very* lucky girl. You know that, don't you?"

"Yes," said Mary. This whole experience still did not feel entirely real to her. She had been honoured when, at the end of last year's ceremony, she had been chosen to perform for this one. Only three girls each year were chosen. It was the highest honour there was. But that knowledge did little to help rid Mary of the fluttering in her stomach. Tonight was far too important.

"Dear girl, there is absolutely nothing to be nervous about," said the old woman. She leaned forward in her chair and clasped Mary's hands in her own. There was a sudden and unexpected surge of strength in those old fingers. "I have seen so many young girls perform at the festival in my lifetime, and none were as beautiful as you."

Mary could feel her cheeks burning beneath her makeup. "I bet you tell that to all the girls."

"No, dear. No. Lying is a sin too. Now, listen, let me tell you something. I was taken to become a priestess when I was six years old, and I spent about ten years in training before taking my vows. So, I was about your age when I became a priestess. From the age of sixteen to – let's say – about sixty, I attended all of these festivals and saw all of the girls perform. And then, when I was too old to attend as a priestess, I was made a Costumier of the Festival. And for the past thirty years, I've been prettying up sweet things like yourself for the festival performances. Think of all of the girls I have seen perform. Just think! Now, don't you think I would get sick and tired of telling each and every one of them that she was the most beautiful? So, you had better believe me when I say that you *are* the most beautiful girl I have ever prettied up for the festival."

Mary was deeply and unexpectedly moved.

"No tears! No tears!" said the old woman quickly as she reached for a handkerchief. "No tears today! Especially not after you've just been prettied up again."

Mary nodded sheepishly before the old woman swooped in to dab away the tears in the corners of her eyes. Then, suddenly, she heard music and knew that the first dance had started. The beat of her heart picked up once more, but now it was keeping in time with the music.

"I'm certain," said the old woman once she heard the music too, "That you dance just as beautifully as you look. You will be sure to capture the attention of Our Lord."

"You really think so?"

"Remember how many girls I've seen perform? I *know* so. He will be very fortunate to have you as a bride."

Mary blushed again. "He must have so many brides by now, I'm sure he'll hardly notice me."

"But, my dear, he will. He will. The brides of Our Lord are very important to him, and to all of us. They are his angels. They watch over his people when he cannot. Our Lord has many duties, and he would not be able to accomplish his miracles without the help of his brides. He appreciates and cares for all of them. He *will* notice you tonight, and he will take good care of you. And, in return, I hope you'll remember a little old costumier and send good fortune her way from time to time," added the old woman with a wink.

"Of course! I will make sure that you receive good blessings for the rest of your days!"

"You are too kind, dear. Come, the first dance is over already. Let us watch the next. It will be your turn before you know it."

Mary walked over to the wings of the theatre and watched as the second performer took a drink from the sacred vessel. The ornate glass was the only thing more brightly coloured than the brides to be, and the eyes of those in the audience lit up when it reflected the stage lights. It was the most prized possession of their community. It had been touched by their Lord.

The Mother Priestess took the sacred vessel away, placing it on an ornate stone dais, and the audience cheered. Then, the band began to play and the cheering faded. All voices were hushed and all eyes were fixated on the girl as she danced. Every audience member held their breath in anticipation. No one dared move.

Mary was absolutely mesmerized by the dancer, her fellow bride. Although she had been worried that watching another performer would make her even more nervous, it had the opposite effect. She was inspired, and her heart fluttered with pride. Mary was going to be the last performer of the night, and there wouldn't be any more of these dances until next year's festival. When the people thought back to this night, she would be the one they would remember the most. That realization lit a fire in her soul. She wanted the people to remember her. She wanted to be The Lord's favourite new bride. But most of all, she wanted to make the old costumier proud.

When the girl dancing on stage finally collapsed and the audience cheered once more, Mary took a deep breath to calm her nerves one final time. As the priestesses carried the body of the girl to the sacred burial grounds, Mary kissed the old woman on the cheek, leaving a colourful mark, and offered her a blessing of health and longevity.

With her head held high for all to admire her beauty, Mary walked to the centre of the stage. She drank the amber poison from the sacred vessel when the Mother Priestess offered it too her. It was sweet and velvety smooth. A kiss from The Lord. And then, smiling her biggest smile, she danced to her death.

Let Them Eat Cake

A blast of hot air rushed into her face, and her eyelids fluttered closed in response. She smiled to herself before opening them again and pulled the cake out of the oven before setting it on a rack to cool. She slid a toothpick into the centre and it came out clean.

"Perfect."

It was a rosemary and olive oil cake that was fated to be paired with thyme buttercream. To some, it might sound like an unusual choice of flavours, but she loved to experiment. Whether or not her adventurous flavour combinations were actually any good, it was the novelty of her creations that kept her customers clamouring for more. Even if this turned out to be the worst cake she had ever made, it would still be completely sold out by the end of the day. That was a guarantee.

What her customers didn't know was that she couldn't taste any of her own creations. Early in her budding career as a baker, she had suffered severe head trauma. And ever since then, her sense of taste and smell had never been the same.

"Ooh, you are looking lovely, my dear," she cooed to the frosting. "I know someone who would love to eat you up."

As she added a handful of fresh thyme to her signature buttercream, she was reminded of those early days after the accident. She had refused to accept her fate, and vividly remembered shovelling cupcake after cupcake into her mouth, her face damp with tears, as she tried to conjure up even just the faintest hint of a taste on her tongue. She had been able to feel that the cake was soft and moist, and that her butter cream was smooth and not grainy. But had she not made the cupcakes herself, she never would have known that they were flavoured with apples and turmeric.

Devastated, she had been sure her career would be over before it had even begun. She had resorted to baking basic, predictable, mediocre flavours. Customers had still adored her creations, but you could buy a chocolate or vanilla cake anywhere in the city. She had had no way of making herself stand out in the cutthroat cake market. It wouldn't have been long before another bakery opened, one that had the luxury of being able to experiment with their flavours, and her customers would leave her.

"Almost there," she said, and glanced over her shoulder at the storage room. "I'm almost finished," she called out.

Thankfully, her fortunes turned when one of her regular customers proved to be a great source of inspiration. After telling her how much they loved her baking each and every visit, she knew exactly what needed to be done to save her livelihood. She made her new favourite customer an offer they simply could not refuse. After all, who in their right mind would say no to free cake?

Dipping one finger into the frosting, she placed a dollop of it into her mouth. The flavour was still a mystery to her, but she rolled the icing around on her tongue to check its consistency. It was smoother than butter and left a velvety coating around the inside of her mouth.

"Excellent. I think we're ready for the fun part now."

She checked that the cake had cooled to her liking, and then she checked the clock. There was still plenty of time before opening. Plenty of time before the slowly forming lineup of customers would weave around the block. Plenty of time to get the opinion of her taste taster.

Treating her creation as if it were a delicate flower, she took great care in assembling and decorating the cake. She carved away any excess with a bread knife so that each layer was flawlessly circular and held each layer in place with a swirl of frosting. With a gentle and expert touch, she surrounded the cake in a cloud of the remaining buttercream.

"Well, aren't you gorgeous. You look good enough to eat." She laughed.

Like her unique flavour combinations, she took great pride in her cake decorating skills. She relied on the visual experience to bring satisfaction when it came to baked goods. Each and every cake in the display case had to look so irresistible that everyone would want to buy one, whether they could taste it or not.

As a finishing touch, she topped the cake with decorative sprigs of rosemary and thyme before stepping back to look at her masterpiece. Lovingly, she slid it into the temperature-controlled display case and gently closed the sliding glass door behind it. She checked the clock once more.

"Plenty of time."

Now that the cake was ready to be sold, it needed to be tasted. Using the palm of her hand, and moving much less carefully and methodically than before, she swiped the cake scraps off the counter and onto a plate before unceremoniously topping them with a generous dollop of leftover buttercream. With the plate in one hand, and her keys in the other, she made her way to the back storage room. The keys found their way into the lock as they did every morning at this time for the past few years. She opened the door, turned on the light, and smiled sweetly at her taste taster.

"I have a new flavour for you to try," she said as she pulled the sticky, crumb-covered rag away from the taster's mouth.

A sickly-sounding belch escaped their icing crusted lips.

"Please," they whined, straining against the ropes that tied them to the metal storage shelves, "No more. Please. I just want to go home."

She smiled, paying no mind to any protestations. After all, who didn't like free cake? She grabbed a handful of cake and icing in one hand while forcing open the jaw of her tester with the other.

"Open wide!"

Hank's Cabin

It may not have been the best choice, but at least it had been a choice. Few people had that luxury these days.

Hank stood by the window, looking out at the freshly fallen snow, feeling only a mild chill in his old bones. Normally, the cabin looked out over onto the lake, but today the lake was buried. The only colour that stood out against the white landscape and grey sky was the hint of dark evergreen trees on either side of the lake. They, too, were blanketed with snow.

"Wish you were here with me, Lacey."

Hank sighed, and his breath fogged up the glass. Quickly, and almost without thinking about it, he wiped the fog away with the sleeve of his shirt. He noticed that the edges of his sleeve were frayed. With a shrug, he left himself a mental note to search for his late wife's sewing kit if he had the time. He wasn't good enough with a needle and thread to fix the problem, but he could at least tidy it up with a pair of scissors.

"Scissors. Yes. Those'll come in handy."

He moved his mental note up further in the queue. He wouldn't mind having a pair of scissors in case of an emergency. And he was certain he'd be seeing his fair share of emergencies.

But the first thing on his mental list was to take stock of what he had in the pantry. There was no electricity at the cabin – Hank had never seen the point – so there was no fridge, but there was always something leftover in the pantry from the last trip up to the lake. This time, Hank was not disappointed. There were quite a few canned goods carefully lined up, labels out, on the wooden shelves. More than he remembered, actually. His son always loved to point out that Hank's memory seemed to be deteriorating. Hank usually begged to differ.

"You might just be on to something this time, Justin."

With a shrug, Hank walked across the tiny cabin to the front hall where his bags lay. He picked up the largest duffle bag and dragged it into the kitchen. It was filled with all of the food items he had brought from home. He didn't want to leave anything behind. It would have been a waste if all the food at home went bad while he was up at the cabin. He even brought the contents of his fridge. Some of the more perishable items would have to be eaten right away, but Hank was confident that he could set something up with all that snow to keep the rest of it fresh. He was pretty sure he had an old metal bucket lying around that would make the perfect makeshift mini-fridge if it was packed with enough snow.

Until the bucket was found, however, it was time for the next item on the mental list. Hank opened up each of his bags, putting everything away. Everything, even items he brought from home, always had specific spots within the small cabin. No matter what the rest of his life was like right now, he wasn't about to let this cabin turn into a dumping ground. No. Everything had its place. He could almost hear his wife chuckling in the corner, telling Hank that he was a silly old man.

"You can laugh all you want, Lacey. A little bit or organization never killed nobody. And you know damn well it's going to help me out a whole lot to know *exactly* where everything is when the scrambling starts."

As he went about putting his things away, Hank thoroughly inspected every room, making sure that there was nothing in need of repair. This was his usual ritual, but today it was especially important. If there were any spots in the cabin that looked like they needed special attention, Hank lifted his palm to feel for any cold air that might be trickling in from the outside. He marked the problem areas with pieces of green painter's tape. Just from looking outside, he could tell that it wasn't done snowing out there. The cabin would have to be thoroughly winterproofed, among other things.

During his inspection, he found both the bucket and the scissors, and he was quite pleased with himself. After trimming the edge of his sleeves and sticking the scissors in his pocket for safe keeping, he darted out the front door to fill the bucket with snow before scurrying back inside, keeping his head on a swivel. He closed the door gently, quietly, but locked it with vigour.

The metal sides of the bucket were so cold that he nearly dropped it before making it to the kitchen. And he shook the cold out of his fingers once it was safely on the ground. Hank tucked the bucket into a corner of the kitchen, away from the windows and as far away as possible from any potential sources of heat, before filling it with perishable goods.

He took a moment to admire his ingenuity before filling the pantry with non-perishables from the duffel bag.

There was plenty of food. More than enough to last a year. Or maybe longer. He certainly didn't want to have to go all the way into town for food if he could help it, especially with all of this snow. And he didn't have any neighbours close by to lend him anything, not that anyone was in a lending mood these days. No, Hank needed to make this food last as long as possible so that he could avoid going into town for as long as possible. Besides, he had no intention of going outside at all unless it was an emergency.

"Better start setting up traps for the squirrels too," he muttered to himself as he closed the pantry door. Squirrels were fatter this time of year, and he could probably get two to three meals out of one of them.

Once most of the tasks on his mental list were done, and Hank was starting to drag his feet, he decided to treat himself to a beer as he sat down in front of the fire. That had been the first task, of course. Once he dropped his bags at the front entrance, he immediately started on the fire. By now, it was roaring beautifully, dancing in the fireplace, and the cabin was deliciously warm.

Hank opened the beer but barely even took a sip before he was up off the couch again. His knees groaned in protest, but he paid them no mind. He made his way over to a locked cabinet and opened it with the keys that hung around his neck. Then, he pulled his shotgun out of the cabinet and brought it over to the couch. As he sat by the fire, letting the warmth seep into his bones, he cleaned his shotgun and sipped at his beer. This would have been a perfect way to spend the afternoon had the circumstances been different.

While his hands were busy with the shotgun, his mind became preoccupied with other things. He thought about his son, Justin. He couldn't remember the last time they had spoken. Maybe it had been a few weeks? Or maybe even longer? Well, it had at least been before it all went to hell, that was for sure. Hank thought about calling Justin once he reached the cabin, but eventually he decided against it. There had never been much cell service up by the lake, so there certainly wouldn't be any now. Justin probably wouldn't even have cell service in the city. Besides, Hank wasn't sure that anyone would even answer if he tried calling. As much as he hated to admit it, it was probably best to forget about ever seeing Justin again.

"I sure hope you're all right, boy."

With his shotgun cleaned and resting on the coffee table, Hank sat back and finished his beer as he looked out the window onto the lake. He loved that view, and it saddened him that this was probably the last time he was ever going to see it or be able to enjoy it. He wiped away a single tear with this sleeve before gulping down the remains of his beer.

Before getting up, he let his eyes drift from the window to the pile of lumber waiting by the door where his bags had been. After his brief rest on the couch, the next item on his mental list was to board up all the windows. After all, he thought sadly as he glanced down at his shotgun, it wouldn't be long until the undead started showing up.

There's Nothing Under the Bed

"I'm a big kid now," he whispered to himself in the dark, shivering underneath the blankets.

He continued to whisper the phrase like a prayer, although he wasn't sure he actually believed it. His mom was the one who told him he was a big kid, so at least she believed it, even if he did not. But a little voice in his head told him that there was still a chance that she had been lying to get him to go to sleep. That was a possibility that made him nervous. What if he was not actually a big kid yet? What if he was still just a scared little boy?

For the past few weeks, he had been hearing a rustling sound underneath his bed. Like something too big was trying to get comfortable in the cramped space. It was a monster. It had to be. There was no other explanation. And that knowledge prevented him from falling asleep at night.

At first, Mom and Dad had allowed him to sleep in their bed, but they soon grew tired of that. Then, they had promised to do a thorough search of his room each night before putting him to bed. They gave that up too. Now, his parents simply told him that he was a big kid and that he was old enough to put himself to bed. They told him that he was too old to believe in monsters and that there were absolutely no monsters under his bed. And that was that. No amount of crying or screaming would change their minds. He was a big kid now, and he was expected to behave like one. That, they insisted, was that.

This was his first night on his own. This was the first night that his parents didn't come in to check the room or stay to cuddle him until he fell asleep. He was a big kid now, and he was utterly alone. He didn't like being a big kid. Not one bit.

He wasn't sure how long he had been lying there, trembling, willing himself to fall asleep, but it felt like forever.

And then he just couldn't take it anymore. He flung the upper half of his body over the edge of the bed and peered underneath.

Nothing.

There was nothing there. Nothing under the bed but a few stray dust bunnies.

With a sigh, he laid back in bed and rolled over to go to sleep. He rolled all the way over until he was face to face with the monster that was lying behind him.

"Can't sleep?" it asked, barring its sharp teeth. "Me neither. I find sometimes it helps to have a snack before bed."

Are You There?

It's been so many years since you were gone.
　　Though not that long at all since you returned.
　　The emptiness was gaping like a yawn,
　　But things have changed and there is much I've learned.
　　Strange happenings surround me day to day,
　　The message in the mirror, frosty air,
　　Toys littered as if someone wants to play.
　　I call to darkened hallways, "Are you there?"
　　It's maddening what I must live with here.
　　I once yearned for you, now I'm filled with doubt.
　　My skin, it prickles every time you're near.
　　The crosses on the walls don't keep you out.
　　No longer caring who stays and who goes,
　　This haunting simply must come to a close.

I burn your pictures, cast out what was yours,
　　And scream my sorrows out into my home.
　　I sprinkle holy water on the doors,
　　You tear them down, your spirit free to roam.
　　A mother's grief, you'll never comprehend.
　　Getting you back was all I ever hoped.
　　The time has come for us to break or bend,
　　My last resort, a trusty length of rope.
　　I don't give up. Attack with renewed force.
　　Your bedtime story is the Holy Book
　　I cast you out, my heart fills with remorse.
　　Your spirit leaves from every darkened nook.
　　The house falls silent. Should I still beware?

I call out one last time –
"Are you there?"

There

At first, I couldn't tell if I was asleep or awake. I was caught in that in-between haze where my eyes struggled to figure out if they were going to remain open or closed. There were pins and needles in my arm. Flexing my numb and swollen fingers, I rolled over to the other side of the bed, letting the blood flow back into the other half of my body.

Before sleep could retake me, I caught a glimpse of light passing through my curtains. Had my bedroom window faced the street, this would not have alarmed me. But when that light shone through the curtains again, I was instantly wide awake. My heart pounded in my chest and all the way up into my throat. There should not have been any light coming through that window. Not in the middle of the night. There were no street lights behind my house. No neighbours. No parks. Only forest.

I fought against the paralyzing fear and shot up in bed, but I crawled to the window with much less speed. What if someone was in my backyard? And if so, what did they want?

I gripped the edge of the curtain but couldn't bring myself to lift it. I was trapped between wanting to know and needing to feel safe. Clenching my jaw, I tore the curtain open like I was ripping off a bandage.

Then, I waited. Hovering just below the window sill, I sat in silence as the blood pumped into my ears.

The flash of light did not return to my window. My action might have gone unnoticed. But I couldn't bring myself to peek, to see for sure. Not yet. I waited for my heart beat to return to a normal, steady pace and gave up when it was clear that it was not going to happen any time soon.

On my hands and knees, I positioned myself under the centre of the window and waited a second more. Then, gripping the window sill, my knuckles white and trembling, I raised my head.

I paused, and raised my head some more.

Nothing.

There was nothing outside, nothing that would produce any kind of light. I was confused. And curious. I was awake enough that I was convinced I didn't imagine the light. Part of me wanted to get out of bed and check the backyard, but I didn't feel like stumbling around in the dark at this hour. Especially if there was someone out there with a flashlight – or something even worse.

But my heart was still beating steadily, and I knew I had quite some time before sleep would come back to me, if it did at all. I wasn't ready to let this go. My eyes scanned the backyard, inch by inch, in search of even the smallest clue. Nothing was out of place. There wasn't even a single firefly. With a sigh, I sunk back into bed and resigned to letting my head fall to the pillow. But, as I expected, sleep didn't come. So I was wide awake when the next flash of light shone through my window.

Without thinking, I jumped to the window and pressed my face to the glass. Still nothing. I scanned the backyard once more, keeping my face right up against the window until my breath fogged up my view. As I wiped the condensation away with my sleeve, it occurred to me that there was one place I had not thought to look. The forest.

Inch by inch, tree by tree, I searched for the mysterious light. This time, when my heart started pounding it was out of excitement. I would not be able to sleep again until I knew exactly what the source of the light was and where it was coming from. But there was nothing out there.

Suddenly, my eyes filled with light. The brightness was astounding, and I couldn't see anything else for a few moments. As the world outside came back into focus, I wondered if it had been that bright before. When it shone through the window those first few times, it was as if a flashlight was waving back and forth. Now, it felt as if the light was coming from my eyes, like my brain tricked me into thinking I had two lightbulbs in my head. And there was still nothing outside. It made no sense. All I knew for sure was that I had to get closer to the source, wherever it was.

Forgetting my reservations about going out alone at night, in the dark, I slung my housecoat over one arm and ran down the hall to the back door. I pressed my face briefly against the glass one last time before stepping outside, leaving the door unlocked and ajar behind me. Nothing mattered more to me than finding the source of that light.

The grass was damp between my bare toes, and I wrapped myself in my housecoat to protect against the cool breeze. The stench of rot hung in the air, and I wondered briefly what could be causing that smell. Garbage day was two days ago, and none of the neighbours had hosted any outdoor parties recently. Maybe there was a dead animal nearby.

My attention soon wandered towards the thick wall of trees that sat not too far away from the edge of my backyard. In the back of my brain, I knew instinctively that the light was coming from the forest. It had to be.

I waited at the edge of my yard, gripping the top of the fence, barely allowing myself to blink. Light filled my eyes again. It took longer for my vision to return than it had before, but now that I was closer to the source, its call was stronger. It beckoned me. I knew exactly where to look for it now, and a churning in my stomach warned me that there would be consequences if I didn't go towards the light. It was far more than a desire now. It was a need, an obsession.

My head turned on its own towards what I knew in my heart to be the source of the light. Everything would be okay if I could just see it again. Then, I could rest.

There.

In the trees.

A small bauble of light hovering about seven or eight feet in the air. Its dull glow didn't look powerful enough to fill my eyes with light, but my gut told me that this was the source. I leaned as far as I could over the edge of the fence and almost fell over. I had to get closer.

There.

Another flash of light.

I was over the fence before I knew it. My feet led the way, taking me from the soft, manicured grass of my lawn to the prickly, unkempt underbrush that led to the forest. When the stars cleared from my eyes, my pupils were immediately drawn back to the source of light. My body turned me in the right direction. I couldn't look away, even if I wanted to. And I didn't want to.

There.

Emerging from the shadows.

An alien creature slinked into view from between the trees. It's lanky, twig-like body had been perfectly camouflaged, but now was illuminated by the ball of light that hung from the thin rod of flesh on its head. Round, milky, white eyes watched me in the gloom. I smiled, and it smiled back.

The closer I got, the more its lower jaw unhinged, like that of a snake. Its lips peeled back over-long, needle-like teeth that jutted out at all angles and clustered together, despite the ample space available. The stench of rotting flesh that drifted from its open mouth became sweet and enticing the closer I got.

Now I was close enough to touch it. I reached up to touch the light, but it danced away from my fingers like a lure on a fishing pole. My next few tries to grasp it were unsuccessful, and the rod bounced the light even closer to the creature's head. I had no choice but to follow, to get even closer.

By the time the toothy jaws were open wider than the widest parts of my body, I was close enough to spot a second light source. It was small, much smaller than the other, but filled my eyes with light all the same. This tiny light dangled from the uvula of the creature. It was just as enticing as the one that grew out of its head. And it had even more control over me.

I *had* to get closer to the source of the light.

He Loves Me, He Loves Me Not

He stared at his empty glass, only half-listening to her drone on about her lysimachia nummularia. A quick and only somewhat discreet search on his phone told him what kind of plant that was, and he rolled his eyes. She didn't notice. When he had decided to ask out a girl from his gardening club, he knew he'd end up with a plant enthusiast, but she was too much. And yet, not enough.

A quick glance around the busy restaurant confirmed the waiter wouldn't be coming by any time soon to ask if he wanted a refill on his drink. He wasn't sure if he could finish the evening sober. Or at all, for that matter.

"And that's why you should never use–"

"Maybe we should cut this off."

She blinked a few times as if she was startled by the fact he could talk.

"Oh. Oh, right. I forgot. You're opening tomorrow at work, right?"

"No, I mean *this*. We should cut this off. Us." He checked for the waiter out of his peripheral. Still nothing.

She, however, continued to stare at him.

"I'm not sure I understand."

"Look, I just don't think this is going anywhere. I think it's better for both of us if we cut our losses and move on."

"You're breaking up with me? Now?" She hoped he hadn't heard the falter in her voice. More importantly, she hoped the people at the surrounding tables hadn't heard. The idea of being dumped in public mortified her. Especially so soon after her last breakup.

"You're nice and all, but I don't think we're right for each other. There's no...chemistry."

"We've barely even gotten a chance to know one another. How can you say it's not going to work when it's too soon to know for sure?"

His face contorted as he chose his next words very carefully. "We've been dating for over a month, and I'm just not feeling anything."

"You're not even trying. I'm sure if you actually took the time to get to know me–"

"We've had plenty of time to get to know one another, and you've been pretty closed off towards me the entire time."

"I have not."

"You have. The only thing I actually know about you is that you like plants. It's all you talk about. You don't share anything with me other than how your plants are doing. I like gardening too, but there has to be more than that. We've been to how many restaurants together now? I don't even know your favourite food. Hell, I don't even know your favourite colour.

"And I have been trying. Really. I've asked you questions about yourself, but you just circle back to your hibiscus, or your creeping jenny, or the new sunlamp you bought. I don't feel like I'm getting anything from you. I can't keep doing this. I'm done."

"But plants are my *life*. I have nothing else that important to me. Why else would I spend so much time with the gardening club volunteering, organizing events, trying to get to know *everyone*? It's who I am. And I was so excited to finally be dating someone who cared, truly cared, about plants and gardening too. You understand me."

"No, I don't. I really don't."

"Fine. I can tell you something about myself. Something I haven't told anyone. Would that make you feel better?"

"I doubt there's really anything you could say at this point that would make me change my mind."

"I grow corpse flowers," she said.

His brain tried to make sense of this information, and he tried to take a sip from his empty glass. He put it back on the table and stared at her. She stared back, challenging him.

"Like the ones from Sumatra?" he asked. "Those big things you only see in documentaries?"

"Not *exactly* like the ones in documentaries, but close enough for an amateur gardener."

He leaned back with a smile on his face and crossed his arms.

"You're kidding. This is a joke, right?"

"It's not."

"You don't have the space. Not unless you live in a mansion. And Sumatra is tropical, isn't it? I doubt they could survive in this climate. There's no way. You just saw them in a documentary like me, and now you're trying to sound clever."

"I'm serious. I have a large basement, and I've renovated it so that it serves as a greenhouse."

She could see the gears turning behind his eyes as he contemplated how else he could poke holes into her argument. He leaned in towards her again as if that would help him.

"But the smell. How does your house not smell like them?"

"The basement is very well insulated," she said.

"And why haven't you told anyone about this?"

"How you think the HOA would feel if they found out I kept that sort of plant on my property?"

"No." He shook his head and leaned back from the table. "No way. You're making this all up. But I've got to admit, this is the most creative response to a breakup I've ever seen. I'm definitely going to remember this one, so I'll give you points for that. But it's just not going to work out between us. I'm serious. Especially if you're willing to make up a story to keep me from dumping you."

"If you don't believe me, I'd be happy to show you."

"There's no way."

With another shake of his head, he decided he was done waiting for their server and placed a handful of cash on the table. He put on his coat to leave but paused before doing anything else.

She waited to see if he would stay or walk out the door. She didn't even realize that she was holding her breath until she opened her mouth to speak.

"I do really grow corpse flowers," she insisted. "And I can prove it."

"You're unbelievable." He sighed. "But I am curious. I still don't think we're a good idea, but I've got to see this greenhouse of yours. And...I guess if you're growing something that cool, I'd at least be open to staying friends. You know, just gardening buddies. But that's it."

She couldn't hold back her smile, not that she tried.

"You won't be disappointed."

When they reached her house, she took her time leading him to the basement. She allowed him to roam around the first floor of her house, offering him glimpses of herself in the decoration, in the trinkets she kept on display. He wouldn't be able to say she was "closed off" after this. Although, it occurred to her that there wasn't as much of her personality present in this part of the house. She spent most of her time in the basement greenhouse.

"Ready to see the flowers?"

"Finally. Were you stalling to try to figure out how to get out of this?"

"Of course not. You know, you really should trust me."

As they entered the basement, the first thing he noticed was that the lighting was brighter and there were splashes of red and blue light hitting the walls from the full spectrum lights. He refused to admit out loud that he was impressed with her set up.

The second thing he noticed was the stench. He had no idea what a rotting corpse actually smelled like, but he was certain that this was as close to the real thing as possible. After a healthy whiff to try to figure out the complexities of the scent, his gag reflex kicked into action, and he regretted ordering seafood for dinner.

"Okay, so maybe you were telling the truth," he said mostly to himself. He clamped his fingers over his nose but that did little to help.

His throat still pulsed, and his gut churned as if losing his dinner was an inevitability.

The third thing he noticed, perhaps a moment too late, were the decomposing bodies lined against the wall. In fact, he almost didn't notice them at all because they were more compost than flesh.

Each of the bodies was nestled up against a bed of creepers and climbing plants that carpeted the walls. They looked like zombies emerging from the earth, and that mental image was enough to trick his brain that the room was sideways. Overcome with vertigo, he collapsed to the ground. On his hands and knees, his fingers burrowed into the dirt and met with both the root network and the bodies of unseen creepy crawlers. He shivered and snatched his hands back.

From the floor, he was at eye level with the corpses. Their bones peeked through here and there, and worms wove in and out between their muscles. A millipede shuffled into an open mouth and disappeared completely.

Cloudy, sightless eyes stared pitifully into the dirt. Flowers of various shapes and colours grew out of the crevasses of decayed flesh. Vines lined the rotten skin like veins and crawled over the nylon ropes that held the bodies in place. Every visible bone was grasped by tiny green tendrils.

One of the bodies was almost nothing more than a skeleton, crawling with a handful of carrion beetles who picked at the bits of flesh that had been missed. There was a part of the skull missing, as if it had been hit with something heavy. A tuft of purple flowers grew from the hole as if this man's head were no more than a flower pot.

He heaved with each new, horrific sight but only vomited when he noticed that one of the bodies was relatively fresh compared to the others. Not quite worm food, the flesh of this pour soul was alive and squirming. Maggots ate their fill from the inside out, tumbling out of the mouth and nose.

"What the hell?!" he said as he wiped his lips with his sleeve. He didn't wait for a response before stumbling backwards into the now locked basement door. A swift kick did nothing to budge the door or break the lock.

"Oh those?" she said as she pulled on her gardening gloves. "Those are just my ex-boyfriends. They wanted to break up with me too."

20 Blackshire Place

"Can you keep a secret?"

His eyes snapped open. Each night, that hushed, childlike voice whispered into the darkness, asking the same question. It happened every single night at 3 a.m., sending chills down his spine, and it had been happening ever since he moved into this house. He had only been living there a week.

Now that his nerves were properly rattled, he knew he wouldn't be able to fall back asleep. And yet, he didn't want to leave his bed. He felt safer in it. Especially when he pulled the covers all the way up to his chin, as if they offered some form of protection. It was the same every night. That crippling fear prevented him from falling back asleep, but it also left him clinging to that false sense of security his bed offered.

The first night he heard the question, he jumped out of bed and went through every inch of the small house with a flashlight and a hammer for protection. The neighbours weren't making any noise, his phone wasn't playing a video, and no one else was in the house with him. He didn't even have his TV set up yet and didn't own a radio. Despite confirming and re-confirming that he was, in fact, alone in his home, he could not shake the feeling that every time he heard that whisper, someone else was with him in the darkness.

It never happened during the day. At no point did he feel like he was being watched. He never would have been able to fall asleep in the first place if that sense of unease followed him in the daytime the way it clung to him at night. Then again, he was busy during the day. It was the back-breaking work of renovating the old, dilapidated house that it kept his mind occupied enough to forget about the whispers in the dark. It was the physical exhaustion that allowed him to fall asleep.

He had always wondered how he managed to get the house for so cheap but just assumed it was because of the state of the place. Half-finished renovations from previous owners could be found in just about every room. Rotting walls and missing floorboards peppered the place. And absolutely nothing was up to code. It even looked like some of the old fixtures and finishes from the early 1900s were still a part of the house. It was absolutely perfect for a buyer looking for a fixer-upper. And the price only added to the appeal. For someone who'd always dreamed of owning their own home, it was absolutely irresistible. Especially in today's market.

But now that he had been hearing the whispered question in the dark for the past week, he began to feel skeptical about the much-too-perfect price. The seller must have known something he didn't. Why else would the house be in such a state of disrepair? He thought about contacting the seller, or even the realtor, but decided against it. He how insane his questions would sound. Who would believe him?

Some time later, after lying in the dark and failing to fall back asleep, he was able to gather up enough nerve to get out of bed. He ran through the house, turning on all of the lights in every single room. Then he waited, shivering even though it was not cold in the house. He waited to see if the owner of the voice would finally show themselves. He waited for a sign that he was just imagining things. He waited for his heartbeat to return to normal.

Nothing.

Shaking his head, he went into the kitchen, made himself some coffee, and opened up his computer to search the address of his home. The first few hits in the search engine were maps and street views. As he continued to scroll down the page, he found an article about a young woman who had lived here in briefly in the '80s before disappearing. The police had arrested their only suspect: her abusive father. There was nothing else to indicate a cause for concern. Nothing to explain why the house was in such rough condition. Nothing to indicate the existence of some dark secret. Nothing to worry about.

As he sat in the too-bright kitchen, drinking his coffee, he wondered if it was all just stress. That's what any rational person would suggest.

He just moved into a new house and was doing lots of renovations. He was exhausted, and stressed, and he was probably just imagining the whispered question. That rationalization seemed to do the trick, because he was soon able to forget all about it, just as he usually did after his morning panic. He finished the rest of his now cold coffee in a single gulp and started the day's renovations.

The current project was the living room. The floors were still in pretty good condition, and there was a nice fireplace in the corner that only needed to be cleaned up, but the wallpaper definitely needed to go. It might have once been white and blue, but now it was yellowed and stained. It smelled of mildew, and the pattern was so dated that he couldn't even tell what decade it was from. It certainly wasn't original, so he felt no remorse as he ripped off the first piece.

He started at one end of the room and ripped jagged chunks of it off of the wall. Both the wallpaper and glue were so old that it stopped sticking to the wall long ago. When he reached the other end of the room, he pulled off one last, large piece that revealed writing underneath. The room began to spin as his heart beat accelerated.

The writing had been scrawled messily as if the writer were in a hurry. It wasn't clear what had been used to write the message. It could have been paint, or lipstick. He chose to believe that the answer was one of those two and not something more sinister. Probably lipstick, he told himself, although he wasn't sure if he believed it. But the message itself was far more disturbing than what it had been written with.

Don't learn her secret.

Concrete proof that this wasn't in his imagination. His stomach churned. Someone else had heard the whispers. He ran to the kitchen and vomited in the sink, bringing up bile and coffee, and heaving long after there was nothing left. After splashing water on his face, he stuffed his wallet and keys into his pockets and left without looking back.

He was now worried enough to spend the rest of the day out of the house. No amount of rationalization could explain what he had just seen, and he needed to put some distance between himself and whatever this was. Part of his brain was still convinced this couldn't be happening, and he turned his thoughts to the task at hand to distract from the problem. This was a good opportunity to spend the day shopping for fixtures.

Store after store, aisle after aisle were filled with more than enough to keep his mind distracted. It was as if doorknobs and light switch plates had the power to banish bad thoughts. He filled the carts, and then his car, with each and every item on his list and then some. Retail therapy was absolutely the solution to his problems.

By the time he got home, it was dark out and he was exhausted. He had, after all, been awake since 3 a.m. and had been busy moving, working, and lifting the entire time. He couldn't even remember if he had had dinner yet, or if he had just gotten a snack at the checkout of one of the hardware stores. It didn't matter. He hadn't had much of an appetite this past week. What he needed right now was to go to bed.

Had it not been for his exhaustion, he probably would not have been able to fall asleep. But his legs were unsteady beneath him, and he collapsed easily into bed. His mind kept turning over the message on the wall until exhaustion won and sleep took him. He did not sleep deeply or soundly.

The next day was very much the same. He woke up at 3 a.m. when the voice whispered its usual question. He got out of bed, turned on all the lights, and drank coffee in the kitchen until the sun started to rise. Once there was enough daylight and an illusion of safety coming through the windows, he got started on the renovations. It was the same routine he had had all week, and he was getting tired of it. More specifically, he was tired of getting woken up in the night and being frightened. He was determined not to let this house defeat him.

The plan was to make more of an open concept living space on the main floor, and to do so he would need to knock down the wall between the kitchen and the dining room. It was a grueling task, but it felt good to be able to destroy the wall. All of his frustration and fear were taken out on those old, weak boards. He even caught himself yelling out a few times as he swung the hammer. It felt even better than he expected it would.

When the wall was gone, he stopped to take a break before cleaning up the mess. That's when he noticed something lying in the rubble. Cautiously, he picked it up as if it would bite. It did not. It was an old, leather-bound notebook. Inside the cover, in small, neat letters, he read that the journal had belonged to a Mary-Ellen Stonebrook. The dates within were all from the 1940s. He smiled to himself, proud that he had found a little bit of history in this old home.

After he cleaned up the mess, he sat down in the kitchen to have a snack and read the journal. Most of the entries were about the early months of Mary-Ellen's marriage to her husband Sam. It was sweet, and it made him happy. It was the first and last time he ever smiled in that old house. Near the end of the journal, his smile faded as the entries started to become more unsettling. More familiar. The Stonebrooks had heard the whispers too.

April 11th, 1943

It happened again. We heard the whispering in the night. I keep telling Sam to ignore it, as if it doesn't bother me. But it doesn't bother me. It TERRIFIES me. I don't know what I'll do if this doesn't stop. I don't know how much more of this Sam and I can take. But I don't even know how to stop it.

April 12th, 1943

Sam is determined to do something about this, but I keep telling him not to. I don't think this is something we should be messing with. If money wasn't so tight right now, I'd pack up and move us into a new house. And then I would burn this one to the ground.

I hope Sam doesn't try anything foolish. I don't trust this place.

April 13th, 1943

April 14th, 1943

I can't.

April 15th, 1943

I didn't have the strength to write this before, but Sam is gone. When we heard the whisper two nights ago, asking if we could keep a secret, Sam answered it! He had had enough. He told the whisper that he could keep a secret. And then he got this funny sort of look on his face. I asked him what was wrong, but he didn't even look at me. It was like he didn't even hear me. All he said was, "Oh, so that's your secret." And then he looked horrified, and cried out, and then he was just gone! Gone!

He's gone.

And that hasn't stopped her.

I heard the whispers again last night and the night before, and it terrified me.

It's so much worse now that I'm alone.

April 16th, 1943

I heard the whispers again, but the speaker has not come for me. Perhaps Sam was only taken because he answered back. Maybe I'll be safe as long as I never answer the question.

But how long do I have to listen to her asking it? How long before I give in like Sam did? And how long until she gets tired of asking?

April 17th, 1943

I learned the secret without meaning to. It's all over the house, everywhere I look. She will come for me tonight.

There were no more entries in the journal after that. He threw it in the garbage along with the debris from the wall. Abandoning the remains of his snack, he got up and walked right out the front door. He didn't even bother to lock it when he left.

He walked around the neighbourhood, battling with his thoughts, wondering what to do about the situation. As long as he didn't respond to the voice, or ask what its secret was, then everything would be fine. He would just keep hearing the question every day at 3 a.m. for as long as he lived there. *That* was not fine.

But, with all of the renovations, maybe he would somehow exorcise the spirit. He was making so many changes and throwing out so much of the old house, there was the possibility that somehow he would get rid of whatever it was that was causing the problem. Best case scenario, the 3 a.m. questioning would eventually stop, and he could live in his house undisturbed. But even if gutting the house didn't stop the question, it would be nice enough by the end of the renovations that he could just sell it, make some money off of all of his hard work, and move on. It would be someone else's problem then, and he'd be living happily ever after in a house that wasn't haunted.

With a renewed sense of determination, he marched right back to the house and got straight to work on the renovations. He tore at every wall, every fixture, everything he could get his hands on, and threw out as much as he could into the dumpster in his driveway. Dust and debris flew through the air, but no amount of coughing or rubbing the dust from his eyes was enough to deter him now. He was determined to rid himself of whatever it was that was haunting him. He would level this house to the ground if he had to. And if things got worse, he could always follow Mary-Ellen's advice and burn it.

He continued to work relentlessly, drenched in sweat and aching from head to toe, until he opened up the walls in a small closet upstairs. After tearing away a section of rot, he saw something that made him pause, something he couldn't quite wrap his mind around. And in that pause, something told him he had done enough for the day. As if watching himself from far away, he closed the closet door before going through the motions of making dinner. He watched as his hands tossed the uneaten meal into the trash.

Lying in bed that night, sleep did not come quickly at all. His mind was preoccupied. No amount of exhaustion would help him to fall asleep now. He couldn't stop thinking about what he had seen hidden in the walls of that closet. The indescribable sight that took root in his mind and spread throughout him like a fungus.

That was her secret. It had to be.

Now that he knew her secret, he was certain she would make him keep it.

It did not happen suddenly, like he expected it to, but slowly. The sensation that he was being watched crawled over him inch by inch, making each and every one of his hairs stand on end. The air around him became warm, like hot breath. It reeked of rotting meat.

He looked around the dark room, and his eyes settled on a little figure at the foot of the bed. She was a pale, dirty child with thin, dark hair that fell in front of her face. Her eyes were nothing but darkness, and her smile revealed sharp, pointed teeth that were stained with old blood. Like a snake, she unhinged her jaw and positioned her mouth at his feet. As she grabbed his ankles and pulled him across the bed, into her open mouth, he heard her disembodied whisper float through the air.

"Can you keep a secret?"

Appendix

Wouldn't you just love to know where these stories came from? I guess I'd better tell you.

1. The Screams: Written for ReedsyPrompts Contest #60 using the prompt "Write a post-apocalyptic thriller." This story is inspired by true events. I woke up screaming in the middle of the night for no apparent reason. Scared the hell out of my husband.

2. They See Me: Written for ReedsyPrompts Contest #64 using the prompt "Write a ghost story where there's more going on than it first appears." I love twist endings, so I tend write them a lot. Although with this story, I decided the obvious twist wasn't the important part but the existential dread surrounding the twist was.

3. Ex: Written for ReedsyPrompts Contest #72 using the prompt "Write a mystery where the detective realizes at the last moment that they have the wrong suspect." Mystery is not my forte – if it was, I'd be a mystery writer – but I've always wanted to try to write one.

4. Costumier: Written for ReedsyPrompts Contest #50 using the prompt "Write a story about a person experiencing pre-performance jitters." As someone who has performed many, many times, I have plenty of experience with stage-fright. But at least it's never been a life-or-death situation for me.

5. Let Them Eat Cake: Written for the 2020 Fractured Lit Microfiction Contest. Who doesn't love free cake?

6. Hank's Cabin: Written for ReedsyPrompts Contest #77 using the prompt "Set your story in a remote winter cabin with no electricity, internet, or phone service." I have a love hate relationship with zombie stories. So much has already been

done before, so I'm always on the lookout to find new and interesting ways to incorporate them into stories.

7. There's Nothing Under the Bed: Written for the 2020 Fractured Lit Microfiction Contest. Honestly, who hasn't been afraid that something like this will happen to them?

8. Are You There?: Written for fun in 2021. One of the lines just popped into my head and I wrote the whole poem around it. Around that time, I was experimenting by using sonnets to tell horror stories.

9. There: Written for ReedsyPrompts Contest #97 using the prompt "Start your story with a character looking out of a window in the middle of the night." Not only do I enjoy combining science fiction and horror, but I adore marine life as well and love to make my monsters look like sea creatures when appropriate.

10. He Loves Me, He Loves Me Not: Written for the 2020 Fractured Lit Microfiction Contest. I had recently seen a corpse flower in a nature documentary and, well, my mind goes to dark places.

11. 20 Blackshire Place: Written for ReedsyPrompts Contest #55 using the prompt "Write a story that either starts or ends with someone asking, 'Can you keep a secret?'" I used to live on a Blackshire Circle. While my family lived there, just about everything that could go wrong with a house did go wrong. Thankfully, there were no ghosts.

Acknowledgements

We made it to short story collection number 2!

As always, I could not have done this alone. Thank you so much to Jasmine Gower for editing these stories. You're an absolute pleasure to work with. Thank you to all of the readers (and fellow writers) on ReedsyPrompts who read my stories and offered feedback. Thank you to Trevor for continuing to be an amazing friend, neighbour, and beta reader.

A massive thank you to me long-time friend Emily Bain (@emilybath on Instagram). We met in kindergarten and have remained friends ever since, so it was only natural that I would ask this talented artist to design the cover for *They See Me*. This cover perfectly captures what I was going for with this collection. And thank you to all of my newsletter subscribers for not only keeping in touch and following me on my publishing journey, but for offering valuable feedback on the cover options that Emily sent me.

And last but not least, the biggest thank you of all goes to my husband Mark. You do so much for me simply because you believe in me and want to see me succeed. I know I try often, but I truly cannot describe how much your love and support mean to me. I literally would not have gotten this far without your help. But Babe, please don't read all of my stories – some of them might be too scary for you.

Don't miss out!

Visit the website below and you can sign up to receive emails whenever Stephanie Anne publishes a new book. There's no charge and no obligation.

https://books2read.com/r/B-A-IKLN-SDHUB

BOOKS2READ

Connecting independent readers to independent writers.

Also by Stephanie Anne

Please Rate Your Satisfaction and Other Unsettling Stories
The Sorting
They See Me and Other Haunting Stories
Coping Mechanism and Other Disturbing Stories

Watch for more at www.stephanieanneauthor.ca.

About the Author

Hello, dear readers. Thank you for stopping by. My name is Stephanie Anne and I am an oddball extraordinaire. My writing assistants include my four cats: Max, Minerva, Finn, and Bubs. Unfortunately, they like to sleep on the job. I have a love for all things strange and monstrous and I hope you do to. If you like disturbing horror stories and unsettling tales of science-fiction, you've come to the right place. Do stay in touch.

Read more at www.stephanieanneauthor.ca.